CU00418896

THE LEAF-SWEEPER

&

ANOTHER PAIR OF HANDS

MURIEL SPARK

Published in 2024 by Galley Beggar Press Limited
37 Dover Street, Norwich NR2 3LG

A CIP for this book is available from the British Library.

ISBN: 978-1-913111-62-5

Text designed and set in Monotype Centaur by Tetragon, London
Printed and bound in Great Britain by CPI Books, Chatham

THE LEAF-SWEEPER

Behind the town hall there is a wooded parkland which, towards the end of November, begins to draw a thin blue cloud right into itself; and as a rule the park floats in this haze until mid-February. I pass every day, and see Johnnie Geddes in the heart of this mist, sweeping up the leaves. Now and again he stops, and jerking his long head erect, looks indignantly at the pile of leaves, as if it ought not to be there; then he sweeps on. The business of leaf-sweeping he learnt during the years he spent in the asylum; it was the job they always gave him to do; and when he was discharged the town council gave him the leaves to sweep. But the indignant movement of the head comes naturally to him, for this has been one of his habits since he was the most promising and buoyant and vociferous graduate of his year. He looks much older than he is, for it is not quite twenty years ago that Johnnie founded the Society for the Abolition of Christmas.

Johnnie was living with his aunt then. I was at school, and in the Christmas holidays Miss Geddes gave me her nephew's pamphlet, *How to Grow Rich at Christmas*. It sounded very likely, but it turned out that you grow rich at Christmas by doing away with Christmas, and so pondered Johnnie's pamphlet no further.

But it was only his first attempt. He had, within the next three years, founded his society of Abolitionists. His new book, *Abolish Christmas or We Die*, was in great demand at the public library, and my turn for it came at last. Johnnie was really

8

convincing, this time, and most people were completely won over until after they had closed the book. I got an old copy for sixpence the other day, and despite the lapse of time it still proves conclusively that Christmas is a national crime. Johnnie demonstrates that every human-unit in the kingdom faces inevitable starvation within a period inversely proportional to that in which one in every six industrial-productivity units, if you see what he means, stops producing toys to fill the stockings of the educational-intake units. He cites appalling statistics to show that 1.024 per cent of the time squandered each Christmas in reckless shopping and thoughtless churchgoing brings the nation closer to its doom by five years. A few readers protested, but Johnnie was able to demolish their muddled arguments, and meanwhile the Society for the Abolition of Christmas increased. But Johnnie was troubled. Not only did

Christmas rage throughout the kingdom as usual that year, but he had private information that many of the Society's members had broken the Oath of Abstention.

He decided, then, to strike at the very roots of Christmas. Johnnie gave up his job on the Drainage Supply Board; he gave up all his prospects, and, financed by a few supporters, retreated for two years to study the roots of Christmas. Then, all jubilant, Johnnie produced his next and last book, in which he established, either that Christmas was an invention of the Early Fathers to propitiate the pagans, or it was invented by the pagans to placate the Early Fathers, I forget which. Against the advice of his friends, Johnnie entitled it *Christmas and Christianity.* It sold eighteen copies. Johnnie never really recovered from this; and it happened, about that time, that the girl he was engaged to, an ardent Abolitionist, sent him a pullover she had knitted, for Christmas; he sent it back, enclosing a copy of the Society's rules, and she sent back the ring. But in any case, during Johnnie's absence, the Society had been undermined by a moderate faction. These moderates finally became more moderate, and the whole thing broke up.

Soon after this, I left the district, and it was some years before I saw Johnnie again. One Sunday afternoon in summer, I was idling among the crowds who were gathered to hear the speakers at Hyde Park. One little crowd surrounded a man who bore a banner marked 'Crusade against Christmas'; his voice was frightening; it carried an unusually long way. This was Johnnie. A man in the crowd told me Johnnie was there every Sunday, very violent about Christmas, and that he would soon be taken up for insulting language. As I saw in the papers, he was soon taken up for insulting language. And a few months later I heard that poor Johnnie was in a mental home, because he had Christmas on the brain and couldn't stop shouting about it.

After that I forgot all about him until three years ago, in December, I went to live near the town where Johnnie had spent his youth. On the afternoon of Christmas Eve I was walking with a friend, noticing what had changed in my absence, and what hadn't. We passed a long, large house, once famous for its armoury, and I saw that the iron gates were wide open.

'They used to be kept shut,' I said.

'That's an asylum now,' said my friend; 'they let the mild cases work in the grounds, and leave the gates open to give them a feeling of freedom.'

'But,' said my friend, 'they lock everything inside. Door after door. The lift as well; they keep it locked.'

While my friend was chattering, I stood in the gateway and looked in. Just beyond the gate was a great bare elm-tree. There I saw a man in brown corduroys, sweeping up the leaves. Poor soul, he was shouting about Christmas.

'That's Johnnie Geddes,' I said. 'Has he been here all these years?'

'Yes,' said my friend as we walked on. 'I believe he gets worse at this time of year.'

'Does his aunt see him?'

'Yes. And she sees nobody else.'

We were, in fact, approaching the house where Miss Geddes lived. I suggested we call on her. I had known her well.

'No fear,' said my friend.

I decided to go in, all the same, and my friend walked on to the town.

Miss Geddes had changed, more than the landscape. She had been a solemn, calm woman, and now she moved about quickly, and gave short agitated smiles. She took me to her sitting-room, and as she opened the door she called to someone inside,

'Johnnie, see who's come to see us!'

A man, dressed in a dark suit, was standing on a chair, fixing holly behind a picture. He jumped down.

'Happy Christmas,' he said. 'A Happy and a Merry Christmas indeed. I do hope,' he said, 'you're going to stay for tea, as we've got a delightful Christmas cake, and at this season of goodwill I would be cheered indeed if you could see how charmingly it's decorated; it has "Happy Christmas" in red icing, and then there's a robin and—'

'Johnnie,' said Miss Geddes, 'you're forgetting the carols.'

'The carols,' he said. He lifted a gramophone record from a pile and put it on. It was 'The Holly and the Ivy'.

'It's "The Holly and the Ivy",' said Miss Geddes. 'Can't we have something else? We had that all morning.'

'It is sublime,' he said, beaming from his chair, and holding up his hand for silence.

While Miss Geddes went to fetch the tea, and he sat absorbed in his carol, I watched him. He was so like Johnnie, that if I hadn't seen poor Johnnie a few moments before, sweeping up the asylum leaves, I would have thought he really was Johnnie. Miss Geddes returned with the tray, and while he rose to put on another record, he said something that startled me.

'I saw you in the crowd that Sunday when I was speaking at Hyde Park.'

'What a memory you have!' said Miss Geddes.

'It must be ten years ago,' he said.

'My nephew has altered his opinion of Christmas,' she explained. 'He always comes home for Christmas now, and don't we have a jolly time, Johnnie?'

'Rather!' he said. 'Oh, let me cut the cake.'

He was very excited about the cake. With a flourish he dug a large knife into the side. The knife slipped, and I saw it run deep into his finger. Miss Geddes did not move. He wrenched his cut finger away, and went on slicing the cake.

'Isn't it bleeding?' I said.

He held up his hand. I could see the deep cut, but there was no blood.

Deliberately, and perhaps desperately, I turned to Miss Geddes.

'That house up the road,' I said. 'I see it's a mental home now. I passed it this afternoon.'

'Johnnie,' said Miss Geddes, as one who knows the game is up, 'go and fetch the mince pies.'

He went, whistling a carol.

'You passed the asylum,' said Miss Geddes wearily.

'Yes,' I said.

'And you saw Johnnie sweeping up the leaves.'

'Yes.'

We could still hear the whistling of the carol.

'Who is *he*?' I said.

'That's Johnnie's ghost,' she said. 'He comes home every Christmas. But,' she said, 'I don't like him. I can't bear him any longer, and I'm going away tomorrow. I don't want Johnnie's ghost, I want Johnnie in flesh and blood.'

I shuddered, thinking of the cut finger that could not bleed. And I left, before Johnnie's ghost returned with the mince pies.

Next day, as I had arranged to join a family who lived in the town, I started walking over about noon. Because of the light mist, I didn't see at first who it was approaching. It was a man, waving his arm to me. It turned out to be Johnnie's ghost.

'Happy Christmas. What do you think,' said Johnnie's ghost, 'my aunt has gone to London. Fancy, on Christmas Day, and I thought she was at church, and here I am without anyone to spend a jolly Christmas with, and, of course, I forgive her, as it's the season of goodwill, but I'm glad to see you, because now I can come with you, wherever it is you're going, and we can all have a Happy...'

'Go away,' I said, and walked on.

It sounds hard. But perhaps you don't know how repulsive and loathsome is the ghost of a living man. The ghosts of the dead may be all right, but the ghost of mad Johnnie gave me the creeps.

'Clear off,' I said.

He continued walking beside me. 'As it's the time of goodwill, I make allowances for your tone,' he said. 'But I'm coming.'

We had reached the asylum gates, and there in the grounds, I saw Johnnie sweeping the leaves. I suppose it was his way of going on strike, working on Christmas Day. He was making a noise about Christmas.

On a sudden impulse I said to Johnnie's ghost, 'You want company?'

'Certainly,' he replied. 'It's the season of. . .'

'Then you shall have it,' I said.

I stood in the gateway. 'Oh, Johnnie,' I called.

He looked up.

'I've brought your ghost to see you, Johnnie.'

'Well, well,' said Johnnie, advancing to meet his ghost. 'Just imagine it!'

'Happy Christmas,' said Johnnie's ghost.

'Oh, really?' said Johnnie.

I left them to it. And when I looked back, wondering if they would come to blows, I saw that Johnnie's ghost was sweeping the leaves as well. They seemed to be arguing at the same time. But it was still misty, and really, I can't say whether, when I looked a second time, there were two men or one men sweeping the leaves.

Johnnie began to improve in the New Year.

At least, he stopped shouting about Christmas, and then he never mentioned it at all; in a few months, when he had almost stopped saying anything, they discharged him.

The town council gave him the leaves of the park to sweep. He seldom speaks, and recognises nobody. I see him every day at the late end of the year, working within the mist. Sometimes, if there is a sudden gust, he jerks his head up to watch a few leaves falling behind him, as if amazed that they are undeniably there, although, by rights, the falling of leaves should be stopped.

ANOTHER PAIR OF HANDS

I am the only son of parents old enough to be grandparents. This has advantages and disadvantages, for although I was out of touch with the intervening generation, my mother's friends when I was born being forty and upwards and my father's contemporaries mostly over sixty, I inherited a longer sense of living history than most people do. It was quite natural for my elders to talk about the life of the early part of the century to which they belonged, and I grew up knowing instinctively how things were done in those days and how they thought.

My mother died aged ninety-six, just after my fiftieth birthday. She had survived my father by nearly thirty years. She was active almost to the last, the only difficulty being her failing eyesight; her movements had slowed down a bit. But really she was, as everyone said, wonderful for her age. She died quickly of a stroke. To the last she was still wondering why I hadn't found the right woman to marry. Maybe she's wondering even yet. She belonged to the wondering generation.

My mother, originally mistress of a great house with countless servants, had moved down with the times like everyone else, each move to a smaller house and fewer servants being somewhat of a trauma to her. She called every new house poky, every domestic arrangement makeshift. It was not until well after the First World War that she got used to only four indoor servants including a man-servant and three outdoor. Somewhere about the end of the fifties she was reduced to a compact Georgian house in Sussex with twelve bedrooms surrounded by woodland. It became more and more enormous for one person as time went on. Her means were sufficient but she couldn't get the staff she needed. A few rooms were closed off entirely. Some years before she died she was doing very well with a gardener to keep doing a token piece of lawn and some kitchen-garden patches, and, indoors, her cook-housekeeper, Miss Spigot, and Winnie the maid. By the end of her life, two years ago, she was left with only Winnie.

After Miss Spigot's death Winnie struggled on, in deep chaos, burning the food and quite unable to shop and clean. My mother wouldn't lift a finger beyond picking flowers; she sat calmly with her eternal sewing, which she called 'my work', giving orders. Up until then I had been accustomed to go down to spend Sunday and Monday with a few friends to cheer Ma up, and she had always looked forward to these visits. She had outlived her sisters and her friends, and she enjoyed company. My own work, a regular theatre column, prevented me from spending much more time with her. I didn't notice dust but I do notice bad food; I must say Miss Spigot, who was already in her late seventies, had cooked very well. Our rooms had always been ready and bright when we arrived during Miss Spigot's lifetime. But suddenly all that ended. Winnie was frantic. I could see that my mother would have to move again. I begged her to let me get her a small flat in London. She was very old but by no means infirm, especially of purpose. 'Winnie can manage alone. I shall have a Word with her,' said Ma, and went on with her needlepoint or whatever. I could have killed her, but Ma wasn't the sort of person you could easily be nasty to.

I decided to stop bringing my friends to my mother's. My own visits were hell. There was a terrible smell everywhere of burnt food, unaired rooms and sheer neglect. My mother's tastes in food were simple and I dare say so were Winnie's, but as for me I like my square meals. The dining-room floor was littered with old bits of toast and egg-shells. The table hadn't been cleared for weeks, the place-mats were greasy. I did my best to help clear up on my miserable Sundays and Mondays. Personally, I'm quite used to shifting for myself in London; in fact, having been brought up with servants, I hate them. Your life's never your own. In London I always manage with a morning woman.

But I wasn't up to coping with a vast house like Ma's. Nothing would disturb Ma's resolve to put up with it or Winnie's exasperating loyalty; she took my mother's part. It went on for a month. I spent all my spare time in employment agencies and on various other means to get someone to replace Miss Spigot, but nothing came of my efforts or those of my friends; nothing. 'I'm going to have a word with Winnie,' said Ma.

On the fifth Sunday I drove down to Sussex late intending to cut short the horror of it all. Amazingly, there was no horror. Winnie had become a super-efficient housekeeper all in the course of a week. As I passed the dining-room I could see the table was laid ready, sparkling with silver and glass, and the table-linen was up to Ma's best standard. The drawing-room was fresh and the windows looked like glass once more.

Ma was knitting. It was almost time to go to dinner.

'Have you found someone to help?' I said.

'No,' said Ma.

'Well, how has Winnie managed all this on her own?'

'I had a Word with her,' said my mother.

Winnie served an excellent dinner on the whole; perhaps it wasn't quite up to the late cook's quality but certainly ambitious enough to include a rather flat soufflé.

'It's her first soufflé,' said Ma, when Winnie went to get the meat course. 'If she doesn't improve I'll have a Word.'

But now something had happened to Winnie. She was perfectly happy, indeed almost blissful. She went around whispering to herself in a decidedly odd way. She served the vegetables with great care, but whispering, whispering, all the time.

'What did you say, Winnie?' I said.

'The soufflé was flat,' said Winnie.

'Turn on the BBC news,' said my mother.

For the whole of Monday Winnie went around chattering to herself. Breakfast was, however, set on the table with nothing forgotten. The house was already in good order before half-past eight, the fire new and crackling. And Winnie conversed with herself, merrily, and quite a lot. I supposed that finding herself alone in the kitchen was now showing. However, my mother seemed to have solved her domestic problem which had fast been developing into mine. I didn't give time to worrying lest Winnie was turning a little funny.

I went back cheerfully to my own bachelor life and regaled my friends with the news of the change that had come over Winnie and of how well she was coping. They were quite eager to come and join me in Sussex again, assuring me they would make their own beds, help with the shopping and generally refrain from giving Winnie a hard time. I thought I'd better wait a few weeks before making up a party as of old. These visitors to my mother's house were either unmarried and younger colleagues of mine who, like myself, had to work on Saturdays for their newspapers, or middle-aged widows who had nothing to tie them to any day of the week. All were very keen to come, but I waited.

Winnie was even more efficient the next week. I came to the conclusion that it was Winnie who had been the guiding spirit in the kitchen all along; she was a good cook. Ma took no notice of her whatsoever, as was always her way, preferring not to praise or blame, just to give orders. Winnie was an unguessable age between fifty-five and seventy, her face was big with a lot of folds, her body thin and angular, her hair chocolate-rinsed. My mother who long ago had been used to picking and choosing maids 'of good appearance' had taken some time to resign herself to uncomely Winnie, and, having done so, she was not now inclined to waste consideration on any further divergence from the norm that Winnie might display.

Winnie in fact could now be heard in the kitchen kicking up a dreadful racket. One evening the noise filled the house for about ten minutes. My bed was turned down neatly. The stair carpets were spotless as of old, and the furniture and banisters shone. Winnie conducted a further brief altercation in the kitchen and then was quiet till tea when my mother went to bed and so did she. I had an uncomfortable night. In the morning Winnie started fighting with herself again, or so it seemed. On investigation, I found her smiling while she argued. My mother's breakfast tray was all prepared and Winnie was about to carry it up to Ma's room. 'What's the matter, Winnie?' I said.

'Oh, the butter was forgot to be put on the tray. Too old for the job.'

'Would you like to leave, Winnie?' I said, somewhat desperately, but feeling this was Winnie's way of saying just that.

'How could I leave your mother?' said Winnie, marching off with the tray.

Well, my mother, aged ninety-six, died suddenly the following week. Winnie phoned me quite calmly from Sussex and I went down right away. There was a little quiet funeral. The house was to be sold. Winnie was still having occasional outbreaks against herself, such as '*The Times* didn't get cancelled at the newsagents like I said,' and she muttered a bit as she went around. However, I spent a last, uncomfortable night in the house and after breakfast prepared to settle Winnie's pay and pension. I believed she would be glad of a rest. She had relations in Yorkshire and I thought she would probably want to return to them.

'I'm not leaving the family,' said Winnie.

She didn't mean her family, she meant me.

'Well, Winnie, the house will be sold. There's no family left, is there?'

'I'm coming with you,' Winnie said. 'I've no doubt it's a pigsty but I can live in the basement.'

My pigsty, my paradise. It was a small narrow house in a Hampstead lane, which I had acquired over twelve years ago. I never got round to putting it straight. It was so much my life to be out late at night at the theatre, then usually some sort of supper after the theatre with friends; in the morning doing my notes for the theatre column, shuffling about in my dressing-gown; then after a quick lunch I would work in my study, or maybe go out to a cinema or an art show, or if not attend to something bureaucratic; or I would play some music on the piano. I worked hardest Fridays and Saturdays, for my last show was Friday and the column had to be in on Saturday at three in the afternoon. And since, until Ma died, I would go down to Sussex for Sunday and Monday with my friends, there was no time to put things straight. Sometimes there would be people staying at my house and they would try to help. But it was better when they didn't, for after one of those friendly tidy-ups I couldn't find anything. Never, on any occasion, did I allow anyone into my little study upstairs. A sullen and lady-like domestic help called Ida came mincing in three mornings a week for a couple of hours, painful all round; that is, to herself, to me and to my cat Francis. Ida took the clean dishes out of the dishwasher and stacked them away; she changed the towels and bedsheets and left them at the laundry. She swept the kitchen floor, making short work of Francis with her broom, and sometimes she dusted the sitting-room and vacuumed the carpet. Francis cowered in the basement three mornings a week till she had gone.

It was not altogether the undesirability of Ida that persuaded me to take on Winnie. At first, I was decidedly dissuaded. The family fortunes had just managed to eke themselves out over my mother's lifetime. I am comfortably off, I have a job, but I'm by no means wealthy. Like most of my friends I wasn't in a position to take on a full-time housekeeper. And for another thing, I had no room. There was the damp basement full of rotting boxes which contained a great many other rotting objects that I always intended to do something about. These included some boxes of my mother's that had somehow landed at my house during one of her moves, and never been forwarded; once I had looked inside one of them; it had held two ostrich feather fans falling apart with moth, some carved wood chessmen the worse for the damp, some soggy books and some wine. On that occasion I threw back the contents into the box, less the wine which was still enjoyable. But I never again opened one of those boxes. The basement contained two rooms, a little dank bathroom and a frightful kitchen. It had plainly been inhabited before I acquired the house.

'I can't put you in the basement, Winnie,' I said, instead of saying outright 'I can't afford a cook-housekeeper, Winnie.'

'What's wrong with the basement?'

'It's damp.'

'I don't need much money,' said Winnie. 'Your mother underpaid me, anyway. Old-fashioned ideas. You need me to cook for you. I can go into the attic and make it over for a room.'

How she knew about the attic I don't know. I had once thought of making it into a one-room apartment and renting it, but it was just above the two bedrooms of the house, one of which was my study, and I hadn't liked the thought of people moving about over my head. So the attic was empty.

The other rooms in my house apart from my bedroom and my study were on the ground floor, a sitting-room and a dining-room with a divan where I put up occasional friends. The only place for Winnie was the attic, warm and empty. What made me waver in my resolve not to take on Winnie was that remark of hers, 'You need me to cook for you.' That was indeed a temptation. I visualised the effortless and good little supper parties I could give after the theatre. The nice lunches I would have, always so well planned, well served; and Winnie was a very economical shopper.

'Save you a fortune in restaurants,' decided Winnie; for it really was all decided. 'And with the sale of your mother's house, you'll be in clover.'

I didn't go into the fact that death duties were taking care of my late mother's property, she having stubbornly arranged her affairs so badly. But it was true that restaurant eating in London was becoming more and more difficult as the food and service were ever more inferior. I just said, 'Well, Winnie, you'll have to settle yourself in the attic as best you can. I'll help you up with your things but beyond that, I'm a busy man.'

'I haven't many things,' Winnie said.

When she saw my house she said, 'The Slough of Despond, if you remember your Bunyan.' Nevertheless she settled into the attic. I paid off Ida and from then on was in Winnie's hands.

It was true my life was transformed. It was amazing what Winnie could do. Except for the study which I locked up every time I left the house and where Winnie could not penetrate, she penetrated everywhere. A new kitchen stove was her only extravagance. I paid no attention to Winnie's comings and goings but it was truly remarkable how she managed to clean out the house from the basement to the attic so well that I saw through the sitting-room windows as it seemed for the first time, and my bed was actually made every day. Winnie achieved all this in a very short time. Within a week I began to have friends to meals, delicious, interesting, just right.

'How lucky you are!' was what I heard from one friend after another. There were a few who would not willingly have taken Winnie away from me if they'd had the chance. My mother's silver and crystal sparkled on the table. Winnie was quite up to serving at a late hour. And her meals were always marvellous. 'Oh what elegance! How does she manage it?'

'Who was she arguing with, there in the kitchen?'

'Herself.'

For one could hear Winnie, after she had cleared away and served us coffee, muttering to herself meanwhile, in the sitting-room, still fighting her lonely battles in the kitchen.

I am a man of the theatre, and this oddity of Winnie's certainly appealed to my sense of theatre. Nor were my friends unappreciative of the carry-on. They thought it was delightful. As soon as she had left the room they called her a joy and they called her a treasure. One of my younger friends, an actress who had formerly liked to visit my mother in the country, had the quick eye to notice, what I hadn't noticed, that a couple of my chairs had been newly upholstered in genuine petit-point.

'You've had your mother's petit-point finished,' she said. 'I remember she was working on it all last summer. The last time I saw her just before she died she was sitting out on the terrace working at this.'

'How do you know it's Ma's work?' I said.

'I recognise the pattern, look, that's the Venetian design, she had it done especially, look at that red.'

'Well she must have finished it.'

'Oh, that's impossible. It's very slow work. For your mother, impossible.'

'Well, Winnie must have finished it.'

'Winnie? How could she have managed that with all the other things she has to do?'

'One never knows what Winnie's up to.'

I was suspicious. But, looking back on it, I think that the truth is I didn't want to know how Winnie did it. It was like admitting you didn't believe in Santa Claus: all those lovely surprises might stop.

Winnie's success with my friends wasn't lost on her. She, too, developed a sense of her theatrical side, muttering ever the more as she served the vegetables or the coffee; and one evening when I had a few guests, for no apparent reason she entered the room with one of my mother's mothy great ostrich feather fans in her hand and gave a performance of a pre-war debutante being presented at court, sweeping the fan before her and curtseying low, with the feathers flying all over the carpet. She solemnly left the room, backwards, treating us to another low genuflection before she left. Nobody spoke till she had gone, but Winnie's dottiness occupied the conversation merrily for the rest of the evening; secretly, I was a little embarrassed. Another time I was having a quiet game of chess with a friend when Winnie came in unnecessarily to tidy the fire. She had cleaned up those old chess pieces from Ma's trunk, they were positively a work of restoration. As she passed us she cast an eye at the board and said, 'Undemocratic.' I suppose she was referring to the kings and castles. But where Winnie was getting beyond a joke was on those days when, after lunch, I sat in my study trying to compose my theatre column.

Winnie at that time of day was usually up in the attic wildly remonstrating with herself. I could get no peace. Finally and reluctantly I had it out with her.

'Winnie,' I said, very tactfully, 'you're beginning to talk to yourself, you know. There's nothing to worry about, many people do it, in fact there are great geniuses who go about talking to themselves. It's only that I can't get on with my work when I hear these arguments going on over my head.'

'Well, I'm much provoked,' Winnie said.

'I've no doubt of that. And I think you really do too much for me. Will you agree to see a doctor?'

'In an institution?' Winnie wanted to know.

'Oh, Winnie, of course not. Only privately. Maybe you need some medicine. Otherwise, I'm afraid we'll have to part. But I do urge you—'

I urged her into going to a young psychiatrist I'd heard of, in private practice. I have no idea what account she gave of herself and her condition but I've no doubt he got some illogical story out of her. She didn't appear to think there was anything wrong with her, and neither, apparently, did he. She refused to go into hospital under observation and he sent her away after a few visits with some medicine. I made enquiries of the doctor but he wouldn't say much. 'She has a few hallucinations, nothing to worry about. She should get over it. Of course I can't diagnose in depth without her cooperation in a clinic.' I settled his exorbitant bill. Winnie carried on in much the same way as before for about a week. She told me she was taking her medicine.

Then she did get quieter. Within two weeks she had stopped her racketing and shouting. I was able to get on with my work.

But slowly the house degenerated. It was like old times, only worse, because, although I began to eat out, Winnie burnt the food she prepared for herself. There was a super-chaos, a smell of burning and old rubbish all over the house. She bustled about brightly enough, but simply couldn't manage.

'Perhaps you need a holiday, Winnie.'

'I stopped taking them pills,' she said. 'Rose didn't like them. They had an effect.'

'Rose?'

'Rose Spigot.'

I remembered Miss Spigot, the cook who died. I remembered Miss Spigot with her specially careful enunciation, her prim and well-trained ways, and how she was said to have travelled with a duke's family all over the Orient. 'Are you talking about some relation of our late cook?' I said.

'I'm talking about our late cook herself,' said Winnie. 'She's gone away. When I started to take the pills they put her off her stroke.'

'By no means,' I said wildly, 'take anything whatsoever that doesn't suit you, Winnie.'

'It's not me, it's Rose. She was a very provoking woman, acting the lady with your mother's needlework and objecting to me showing off in front of company. But she was a good cook-housekeeper, she's a good manager, and I can't cope alone with all the mess. She was another pair of hands.'

'Definitely, you should stop the pills,' I said. 'Wouldn't you like me to have another word with the doctor?'

'Certainly not,' said Winnie. 'There was nothing wrong with the doctor.'

I had to go away for a week to a theatre festival in the north. I was glad to go, notwithstanding my crumpled shirts and unwashed socks crammed into my bag. I felt I could face the problem of Winnie better after a break.

When I got back, as I put my key in the door, I knew something had happened by the fact that my old brass name-plate was twinkling and by the sound of Winnie's voice from the back of the house raised in argument.

Only Winnie was in the kitchen when I put my head round the door. 'Rose is back,' said Winnie.

I could see what she meant. The house was clean and shining; my supper that night was excellent.

But it was all too much for my no doubt weak character. I thought it over for a bit and finally persuaded Winnie to retire. She went back to Yorkshire, accompanied by Miss Spigot or not I don't know. My house is the pigsty of old. My friends are awfully good to me and I dine out a lot. The stuff that used to moulder in the basement is now rotting in the attic. Nobody combs Francis the cat, but he doesn't mind. When I'm on my own I can always sit down among the dust and the litter, and play the piano.